Party Time with Old King Cole

Characters

Narrator

Old King Cole

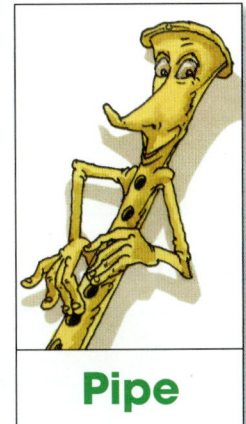
Pipe

Fiddler 1

Fiddler 2

Fiddler 3

Setting

Old King Cole's castle in the middle of the night

Picture Words

calling

fiddlers

Sight Words

| am | coming | he | I |
| just | play | want | was |

Enrichment Words

merry

rare

soul

time

**Narrator:** Old King Cole was a merry old soul.

**Old King Cole:** Ha, ha, ha. Ho, ho, ho.

 **Narrator:** A merry old soul was he.

 **King:** I am very merry. Ha, ha, ha. Ho, ho, ho.

 **King:** Go, Fiddlers, go!

 **Fiddler 1:** Da-da-da.

 **Fiddler 2:** La-la-la.

Fiddler 3: Deet-deet-deet and a zeet-zeet-zeet.

King: Ha, ha, ha and a ho, ho, ho! Yeah, man!

Narrator: Oh there's none so rare as can compare with King Cole and his fiddlers three.

 **Pipe:** I am here, King.

 **King:** Hi, Pipe. You are just in time. Be in the party!

The End